Mesopotamia for Kids Ziggurat Edition

Children's Ancient History

Speedy Publishing LLC
40 E. Main St. #1156
Newark, DE 19711
www.speedypublishing.com

Have you heard about the “Cradle of Civilization”?

Let's get to know one of the amazing ancient regions if the world. Let's explore Mesopotamia, "the land between two rivers".

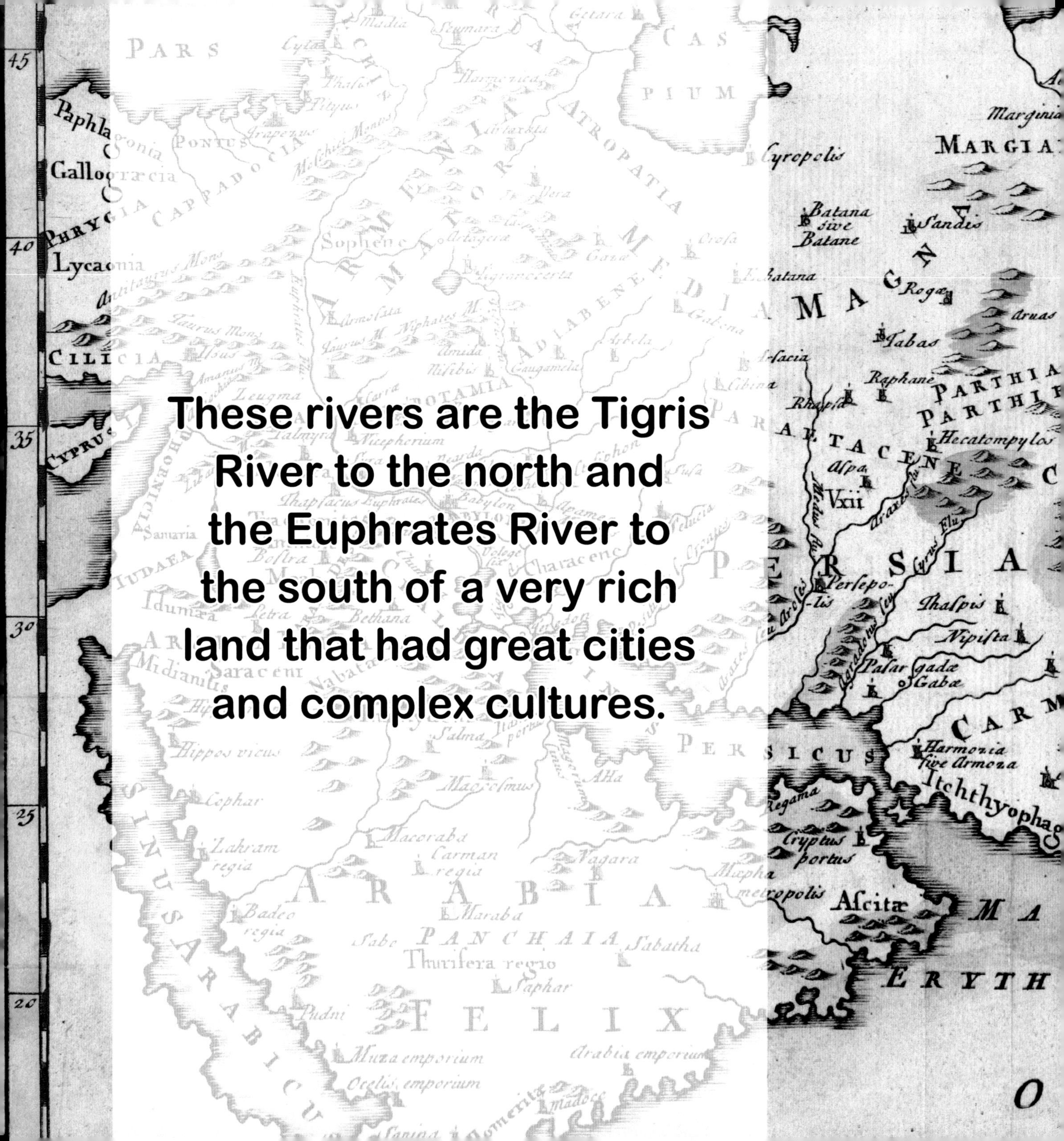

These rivers are the Tigris River to the north and the Euphrates River to the south of a very rich land that had great cities and complex cultures.

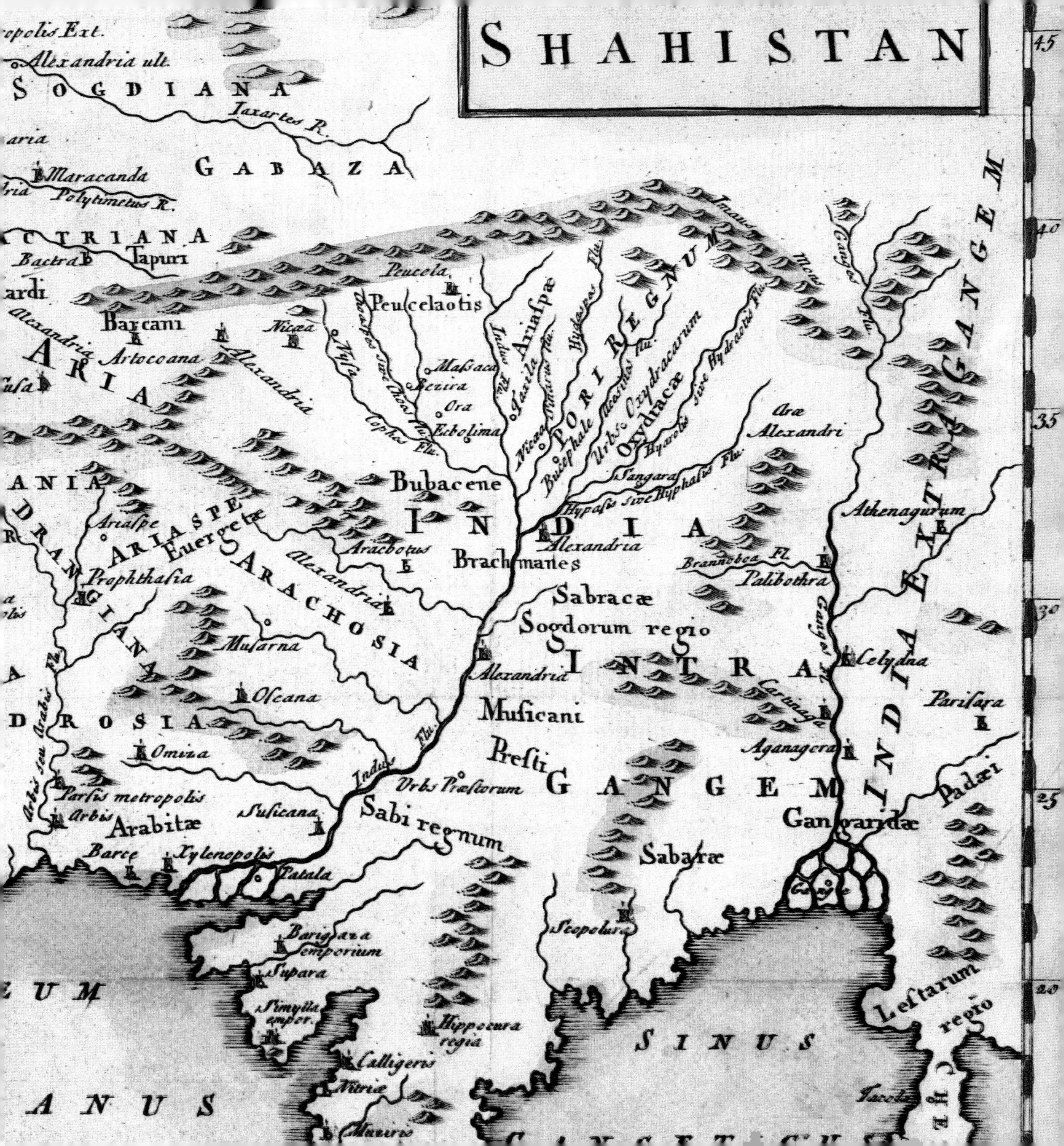

SHAHISTAN

ropolis Ext.
Alexandria ult.
SOGDIANA
Iaxartes R.
aria
GABAZA
Maracanda
ria
Polytimetus R.
ACTRIANA
Bactra
Tapuri
ardi
Imaus
Mons
Peucela
Peucelaotis
Barcani
Nicæa
Alexandria
ARIA
Artocoana
Alexandria
Cusa
Nysa
Choaspes sive Choas Flu.
Massaca
Bezira
Ora
Cophes Flu.
Ecbolima
Indus Flu.
Taxila
Ariaspæ
Nicæa
Suaßus Flu.
Hydaspes Flu.
PORI REGNUM
Bucephale
Acesines Flu.
Urbs Oxydracarum
Oxydracæ
Hydraotis sive Hydraotes Flu.
Hyarotis
Gange Flu.
Aræ
Alexandri
Sangara
Hypasis sive Hyphasis Flu.
ANIA
Bubacene
INDIA
Ariaspe
ARIASPE
Euergetæ
DRANGIANA
Prophthasia
ARACHOSIA
Aracbotus
Alexandria
Alexandria
Brachmanes
Brannoboa Fl.
Palibothra
Athenagurum
INDIA EXTRA GANGEM
Sabracæ
Sogdorum regio
Musarna
INTRA
Alexandria
Gangæs Fl.
Celydna
Oscana
Musicani
Cartinaga
Parisara
DROSIA
Omiza
Presti
Aganagera
Indus Flu.
Arbis seu Arabis Flu.
Urbs Præstorum
GANGEM
Padæi
Parsis metropolis
Arbis
Arabitæ
Susicana
Sabi regnum
Gangaridæ
Barce
Xylenopolis
Patala
Sabaræ
Ganges
Barigaza
emporium
Scopolura
Supara
Lestarum
regio
EUM
Simylla
empor.
Hippocura
regia
SINUS
Calligeris
Nitriæ
ANUS
Tacola
Muziris
GANGETICUS
CHE

45
40
35
30
25
20

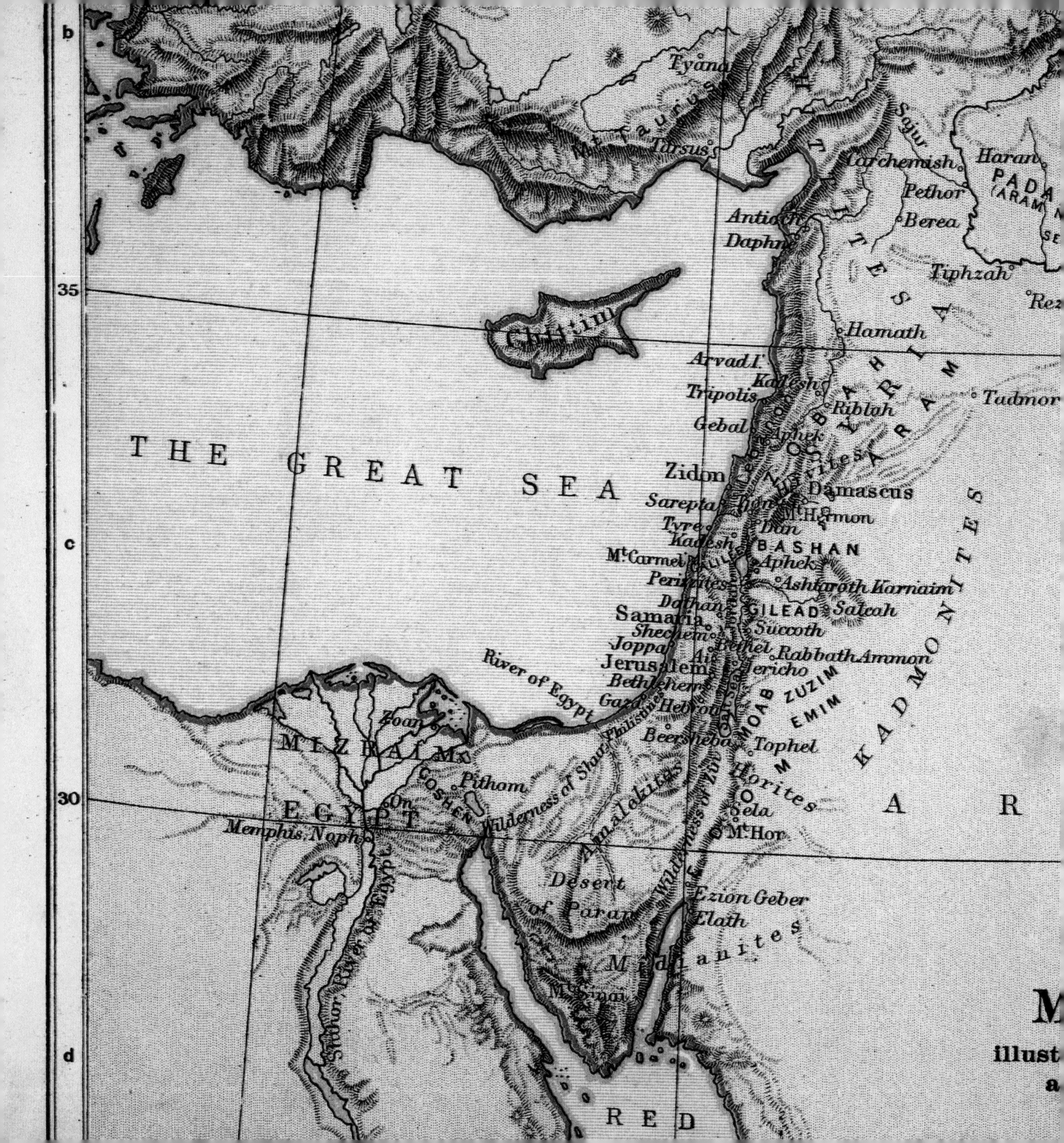

b
35
c
30
d
Tyana
Mt. Taurus
Tarsus
Sajur
Carchemish
Haran
PADA
(ARAM
Pethor
Berea
Antioch
Daphne
Tiphzah
Hamath
Chittim
THE GREAT SEA
Arvad I.
Kadesh
Tripolis
Riblah
Tadmor
Gebal
Aphek
ARAM
Zidon
Damascus
Sarepta
Mt. Hermon
Tyre
Dan
Kadesh
BASHAN
Mt. Carmel
Aphek
Perizzites
Ashtaroth Karnaim
Dothan
GILEAD
Salcah
Samaria
Succoth
Shechem
Joppa
Bethel
Rabbath Ammon
Jerusalem
Jericho
River of Egypt
Bethlehem
ZUZIM
Gaza
Hebron
MOAB
EMIM
Philistines
KADMONITES
Zoan
Beersheba
Tophel
MIZRAIM
Pithom
GOSHEN
Wilderness of Shur
Amalekites
Horites
EGYPT
On
Sela
A R
Memphis, Noph
Wilderness of Zin
Mt. Hor
Desert of Paran
Ezion Geber
Elath
River of Egypt
Sihor
Midianites
Mt. Sinai
RED
M
illust
a

The area was called "The Fertile Crescent". Mesopotamia measured about 300 miles long and 150 miles wide.

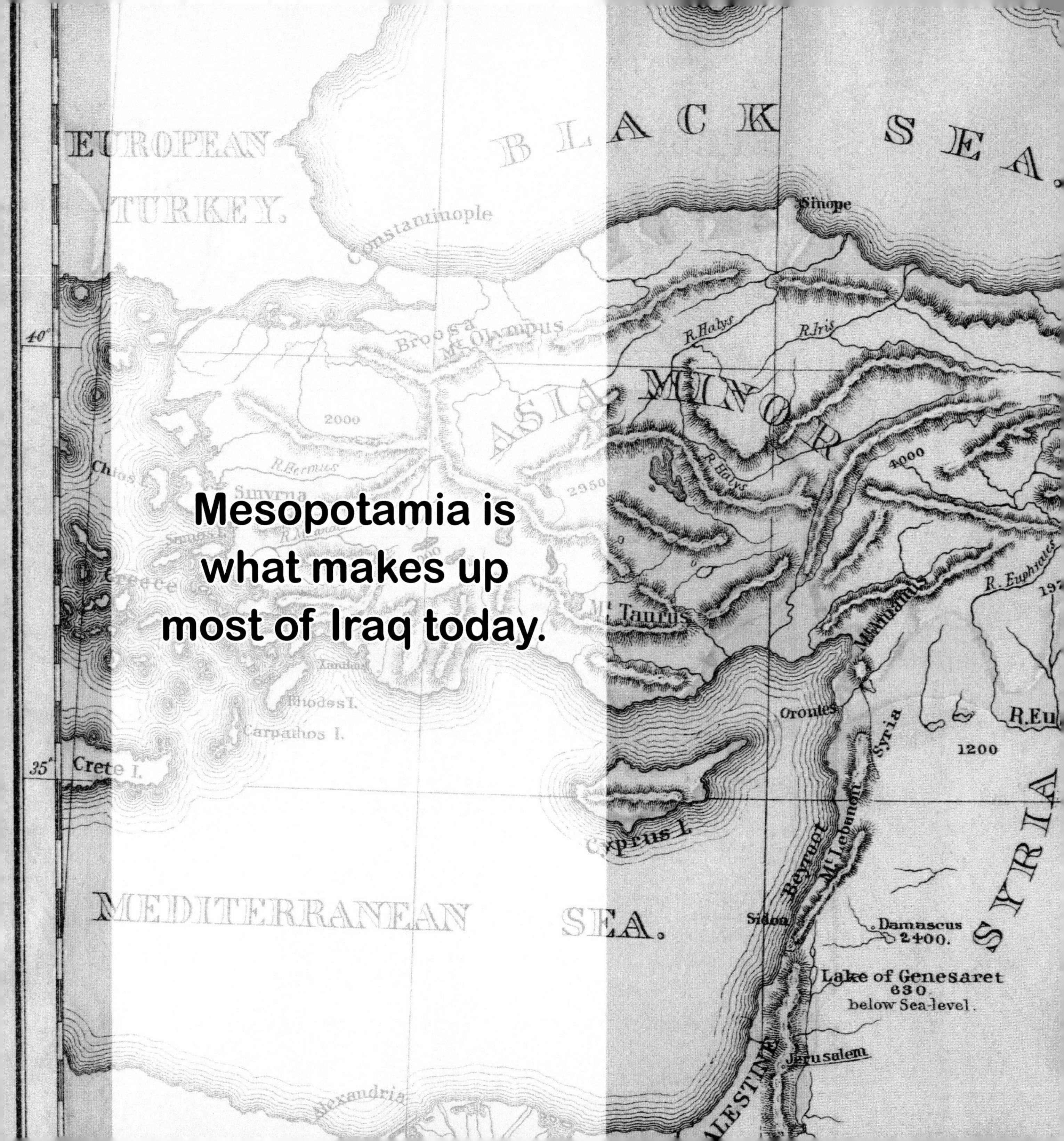

Mesopotamia is what makes up most of Iraq today.

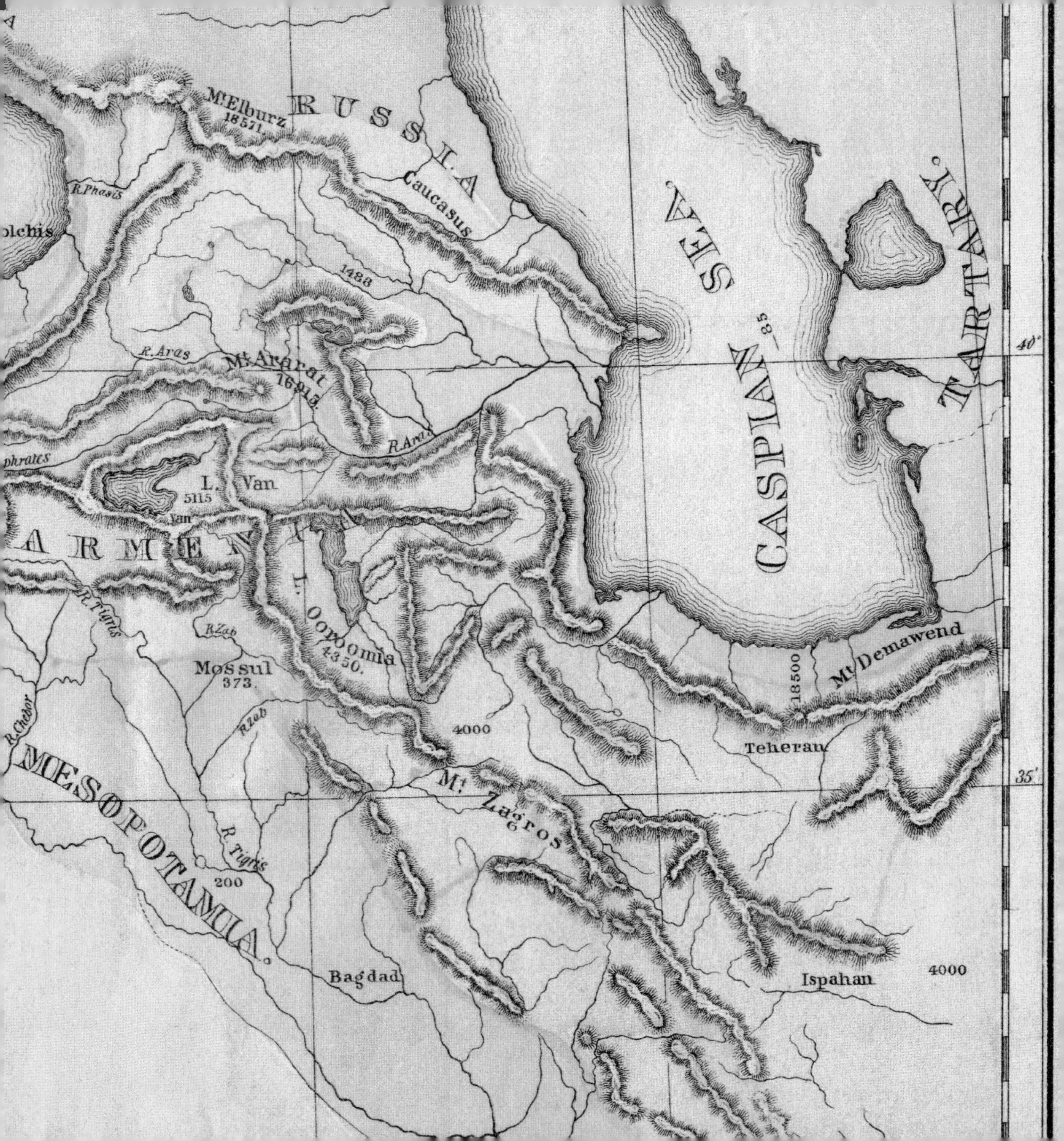

RUSSIA
Mt. Elburz
18571
Caucasus
R. Phasis
olchis
1488
R. Aras
Mt. Ararat
16915
R. Aras
phrates
L. Van
5115
Van
ARMEN
R. Tigris
R. Zab
Mossul
373
Ooroomia
4350
4000
R. Zab
R. Chebor
MESOPOTAMIA
Mt. Zagros
6
R. Tigris
200
Bagdad
CASPIAN SEA
85
TARTARY
40°
Mt. Demawend
18500
Teheran
35°
Ispahan
4000

Why should we study about Ancient Mesopotamia? What's interesting about this ancient region? Mesopotamia is considered as the first human civilization.

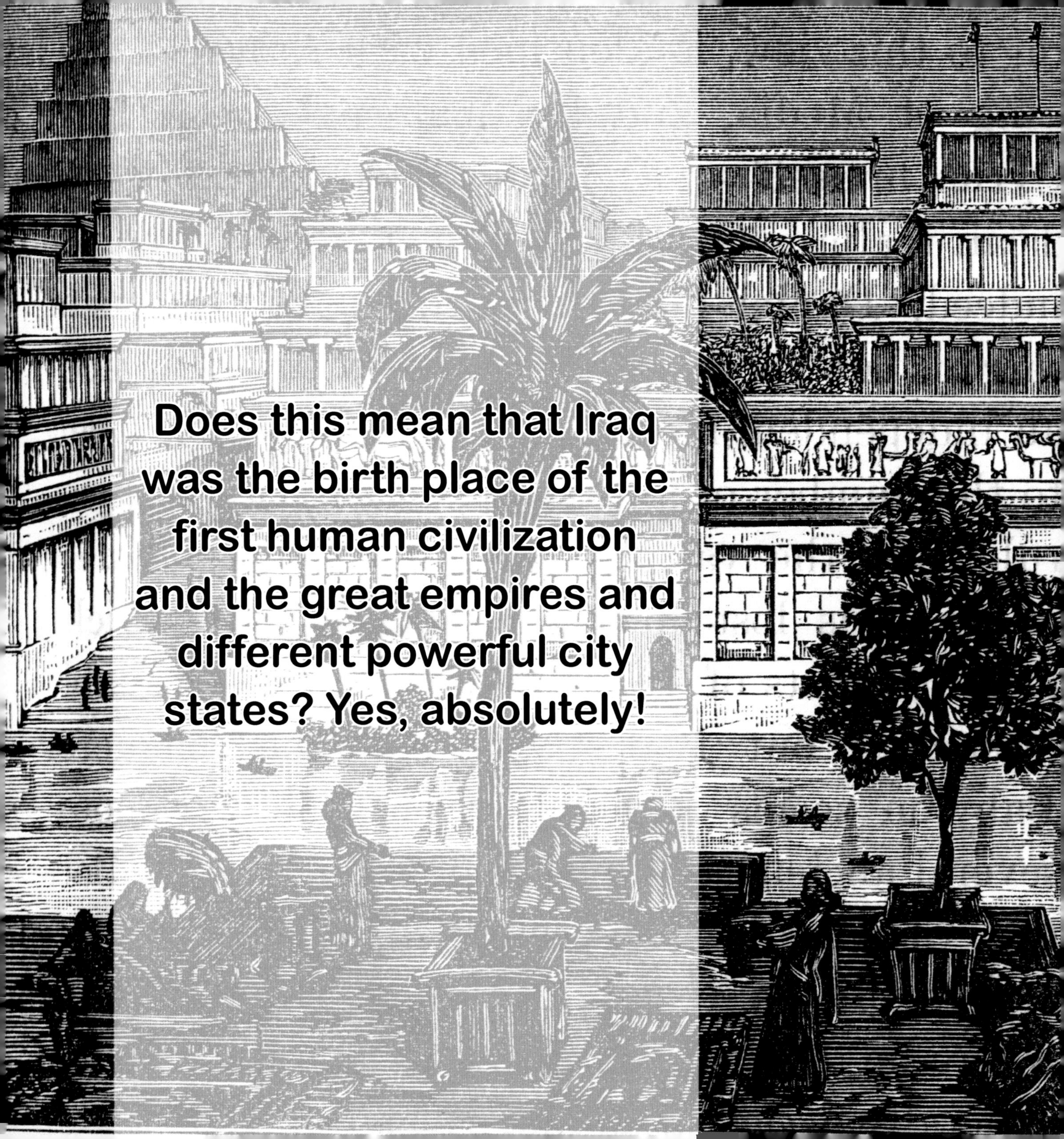

Does this mean that Iraq was the birth place of the first human civilization and the great empires and different powerful city states? Yes, absolutely!

Ancient Mesopotamia is where people first developing writing and reading. It was the first area governed by written laws.

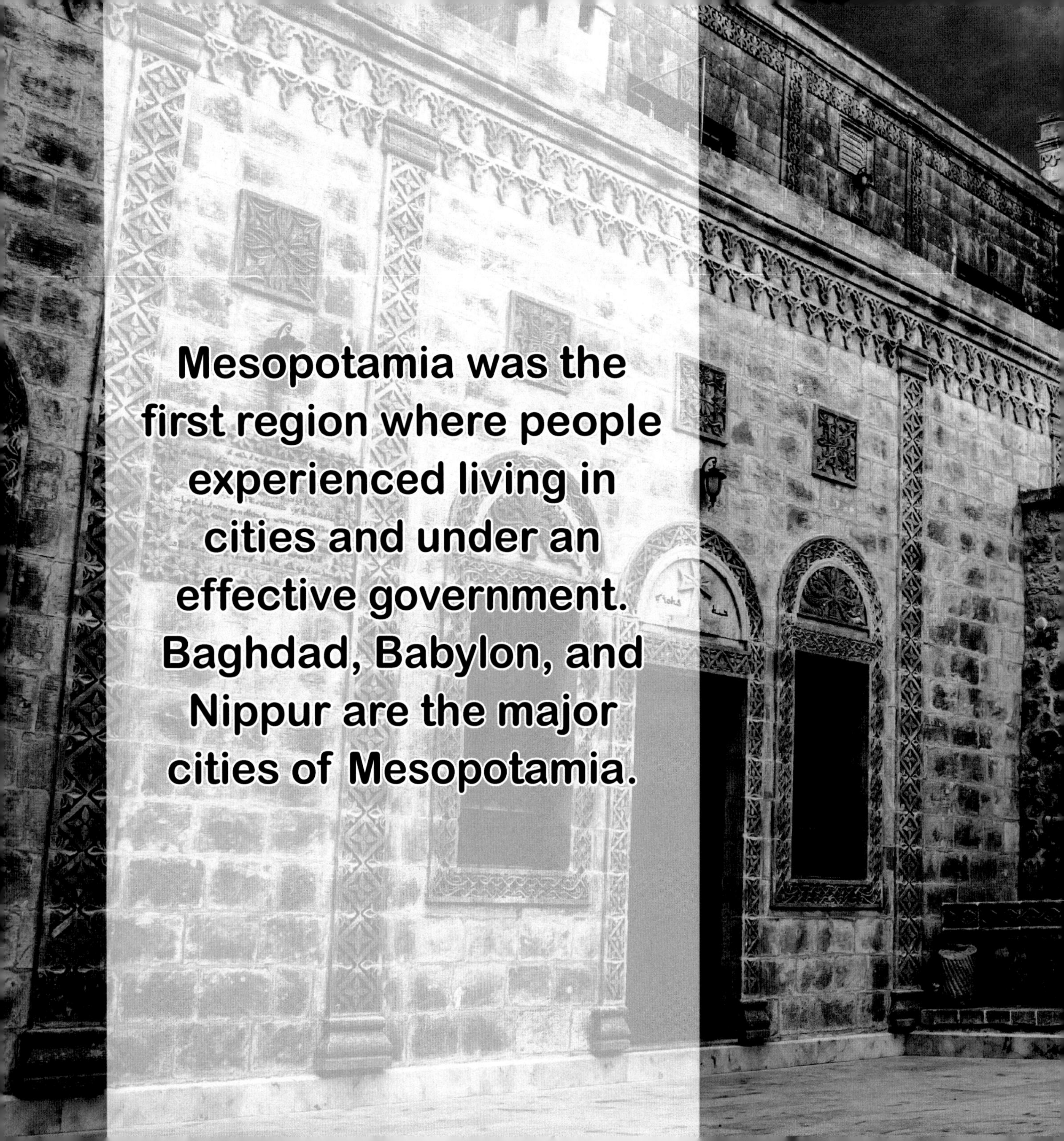
Mesopotamia was the first region where people experienced living in cities and under an effective government. Baghdad, Babylon, and Nippur are the major cities of Mesopotamia.

Baghdad is in the middle of Iraq. Babylon is situated along the Euphrates River while Nippur was in the southern part of Babylon. Babylon was the capital city of Mesopotamia.

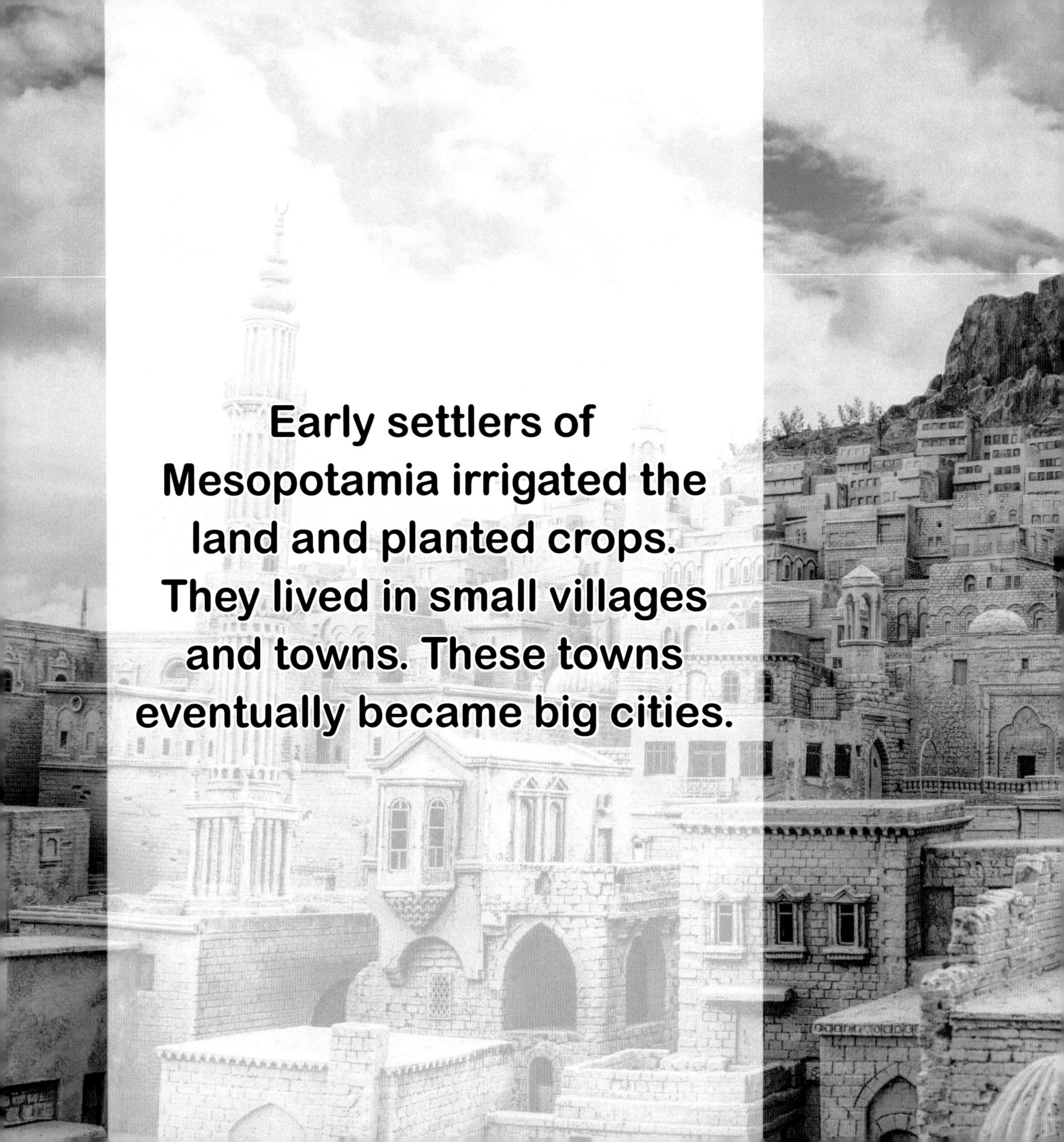

Early settlers of Mesopotamia irrigated the land and planted crops. They lived in small villages and towns. These towns eventually became big cities.

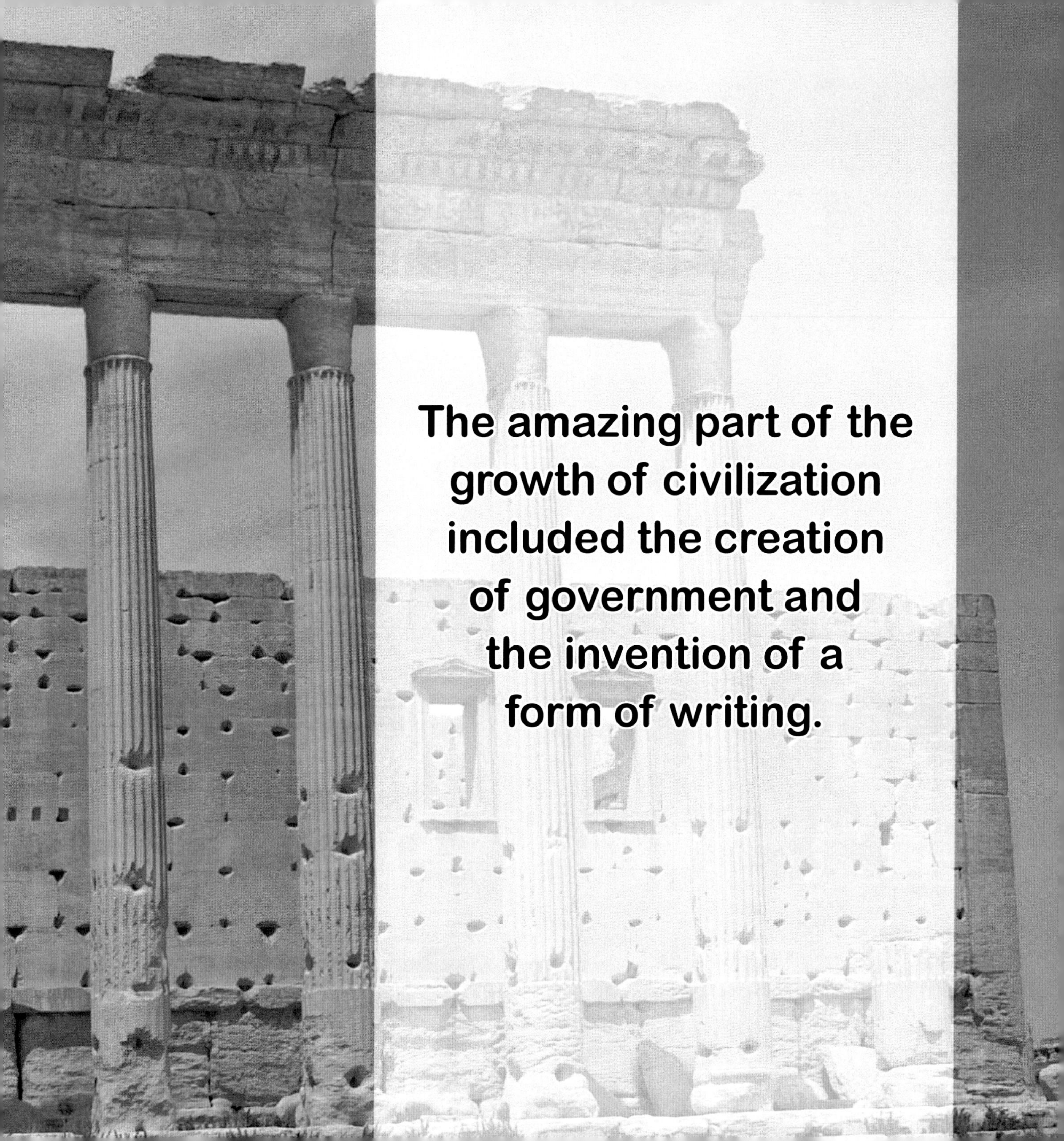
The amazing part of the growth of civilization included the creation of government and the invention of a form of writing.

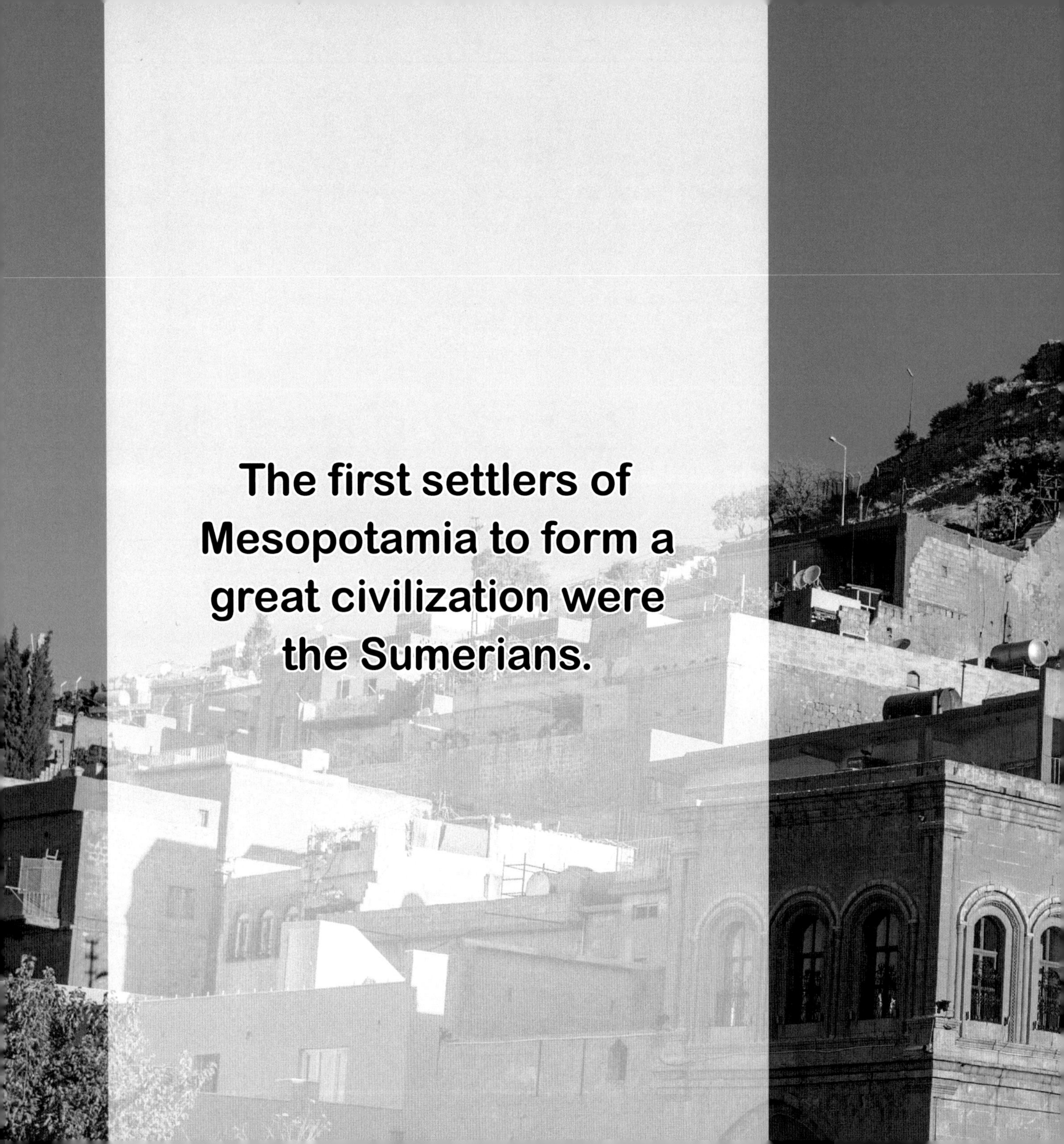

The first settlers of Mesopotamia to form a great civilization were the Sumerians.

The Sumerians were organized according to different city-states which were ruled by kings.

The Akkadians were considered as the second civilization of Mesopotamia.

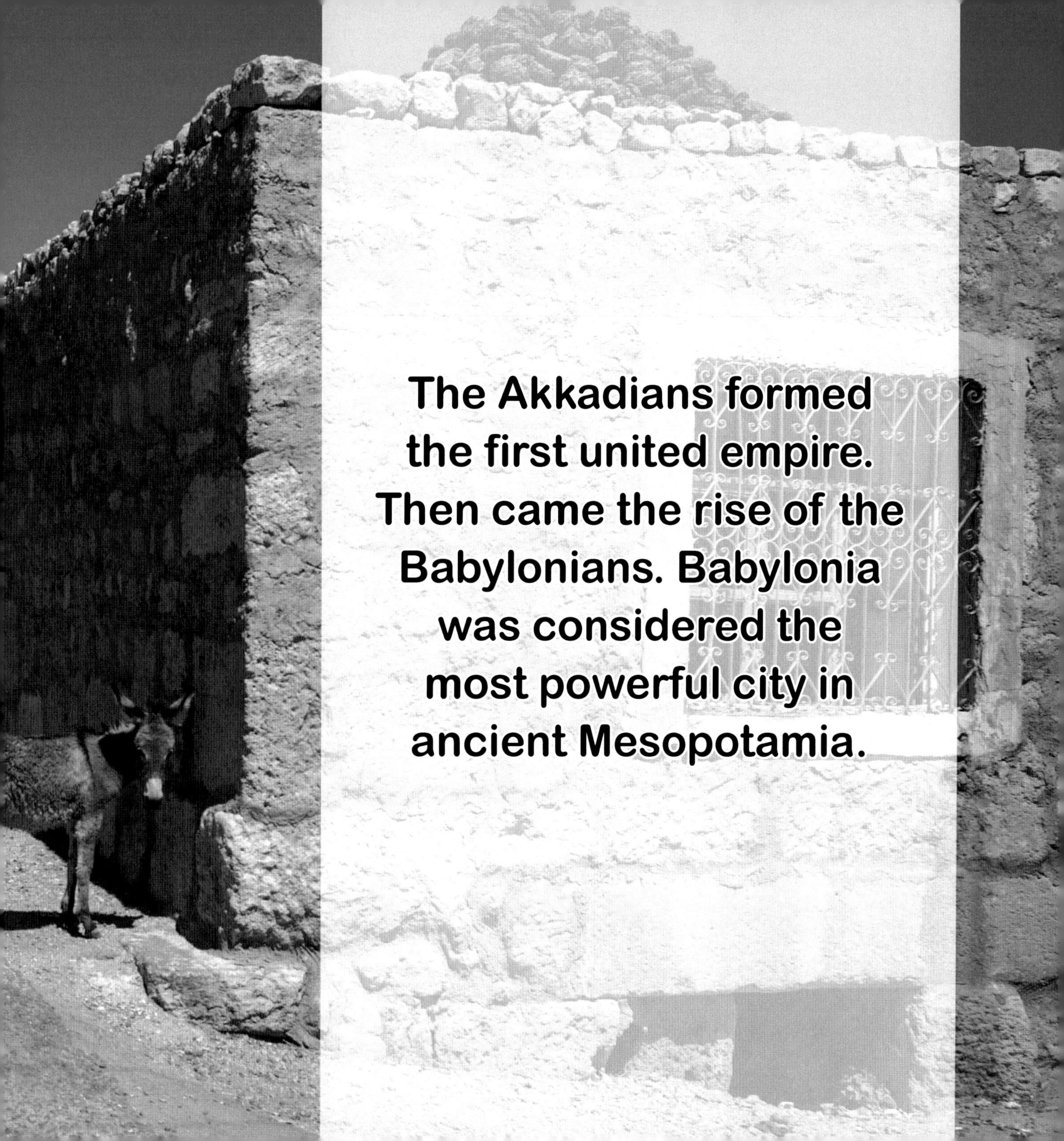

The Akkadians formed the first united empire. Then came the rise of the Babylonians. Babylonia was considered the most powerful city in ancient Mesopotamia.

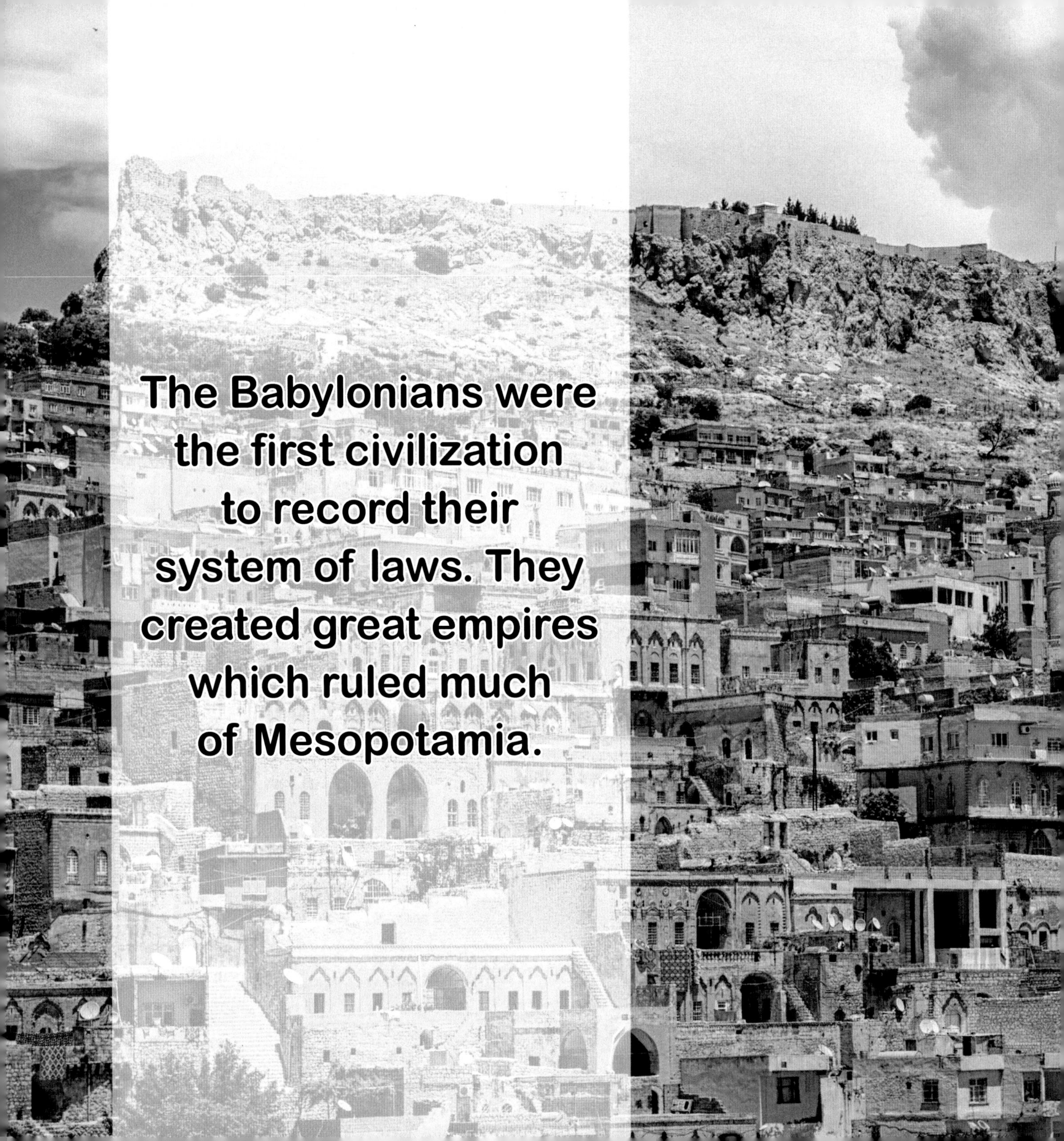

The Babylonians were the first civilization to record their system of laws. They created great empires which ruled much of Mesopotamia.

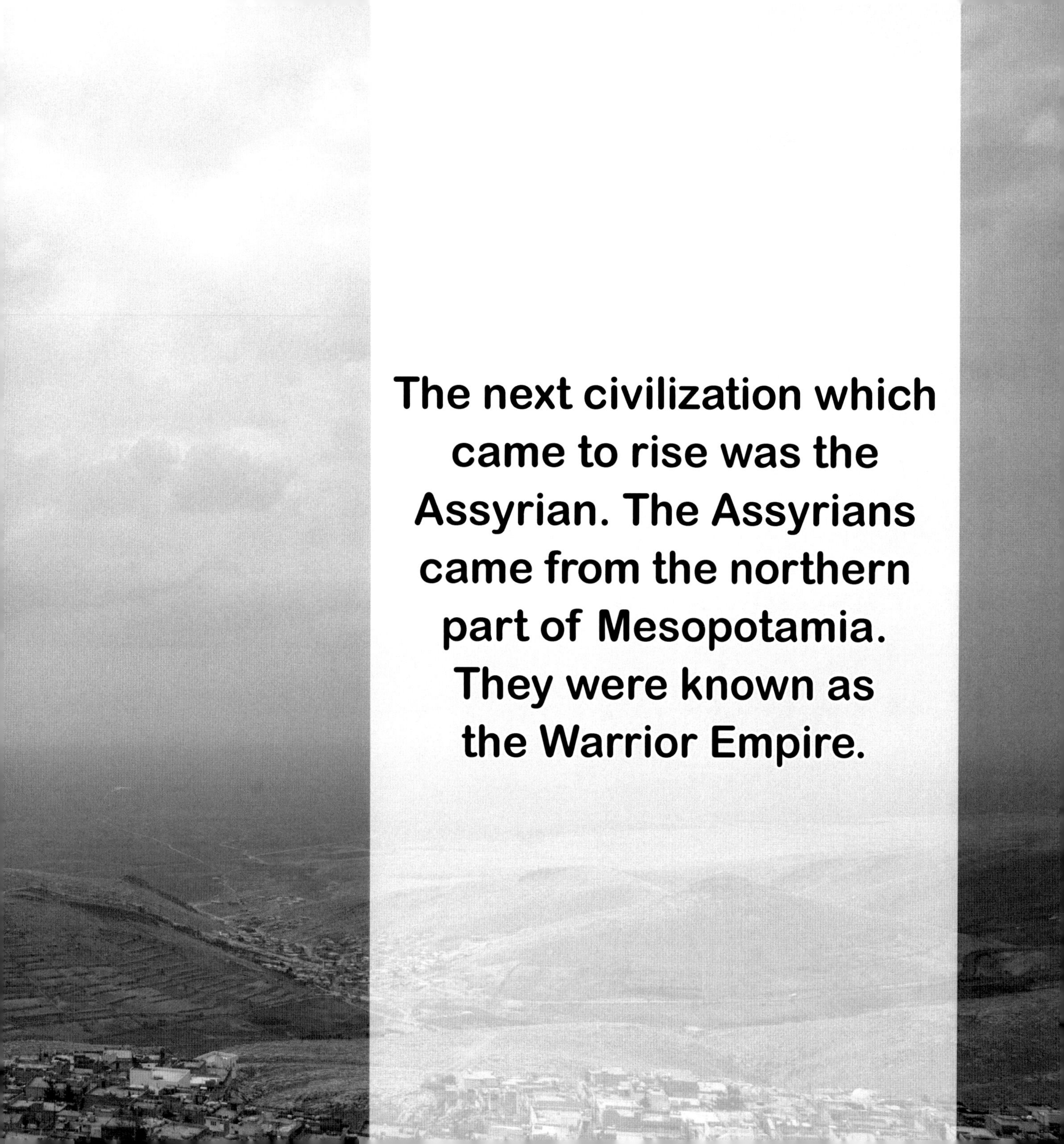

The next civilization which came to rise was the Assyrian. The Assyrians came from the northern part of Mesopotamia. They were known as the Warrior Empire.

The Persians were the last of the Mesopotamian empires to conquer much of the Middle East. Persia conquered Mesopotamia and ended the rule of the Assyrians and Babylonians.

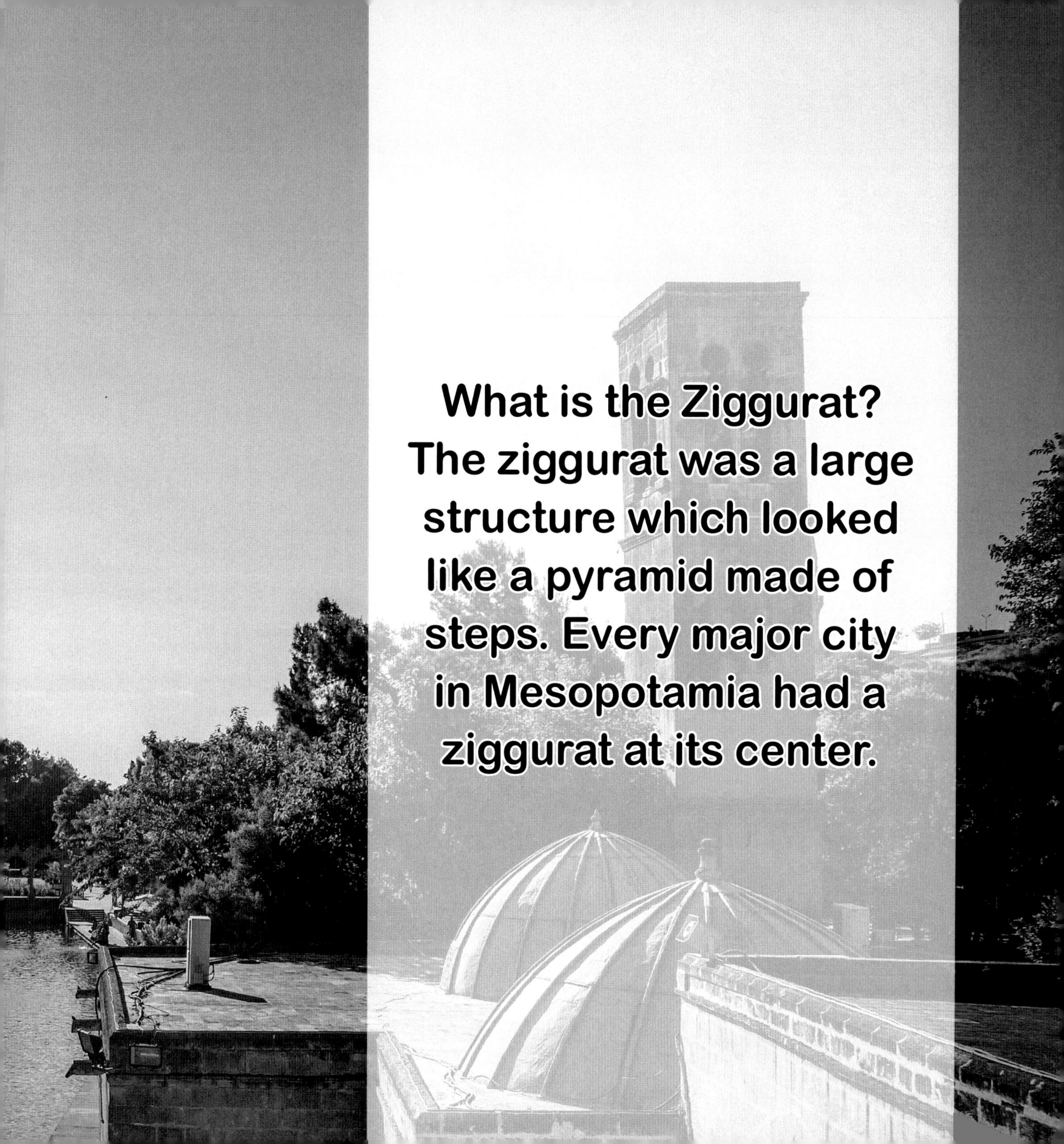

What is the Ziggurat?
The ziggurat was a large structure which looked like a pyramid made of steps. Every major city in Mesopotamia had a ziggurat at its center.

The ziggurat was built in honor of their main god. The Sumerians were the first empire to build a ziggurat. This practice was followed by other civilizations.

The largest ziggurat was built in the city of Babylon and rose nearly 300 feet. It was a seven-story structure built by King Nebuchadnezzar II.

The ziggurats were the great pyramids and were the spiritual heart of ancient Mesopotamia.

The largest ziggurat to survive is 78 feet high. It was built at Chogha Zambil in Elam around 1200 BC.

Ziggurat means a raised area. It was a very broad platform at the bottom and ascended to smaller structures. The top of the structure was flat and a temple was found there.

Only the priests were allowed to go there. The ziggurats were mainly used as temples for the gods in the city. It was the key connection between the Mesopotamians and their local gods.

During the 3rd millennium BC, the most significant Sumerian city-state in ancient Mesopotamia was the city of Ur. This ancient city took pride of the Great Ziggurat of Ur.

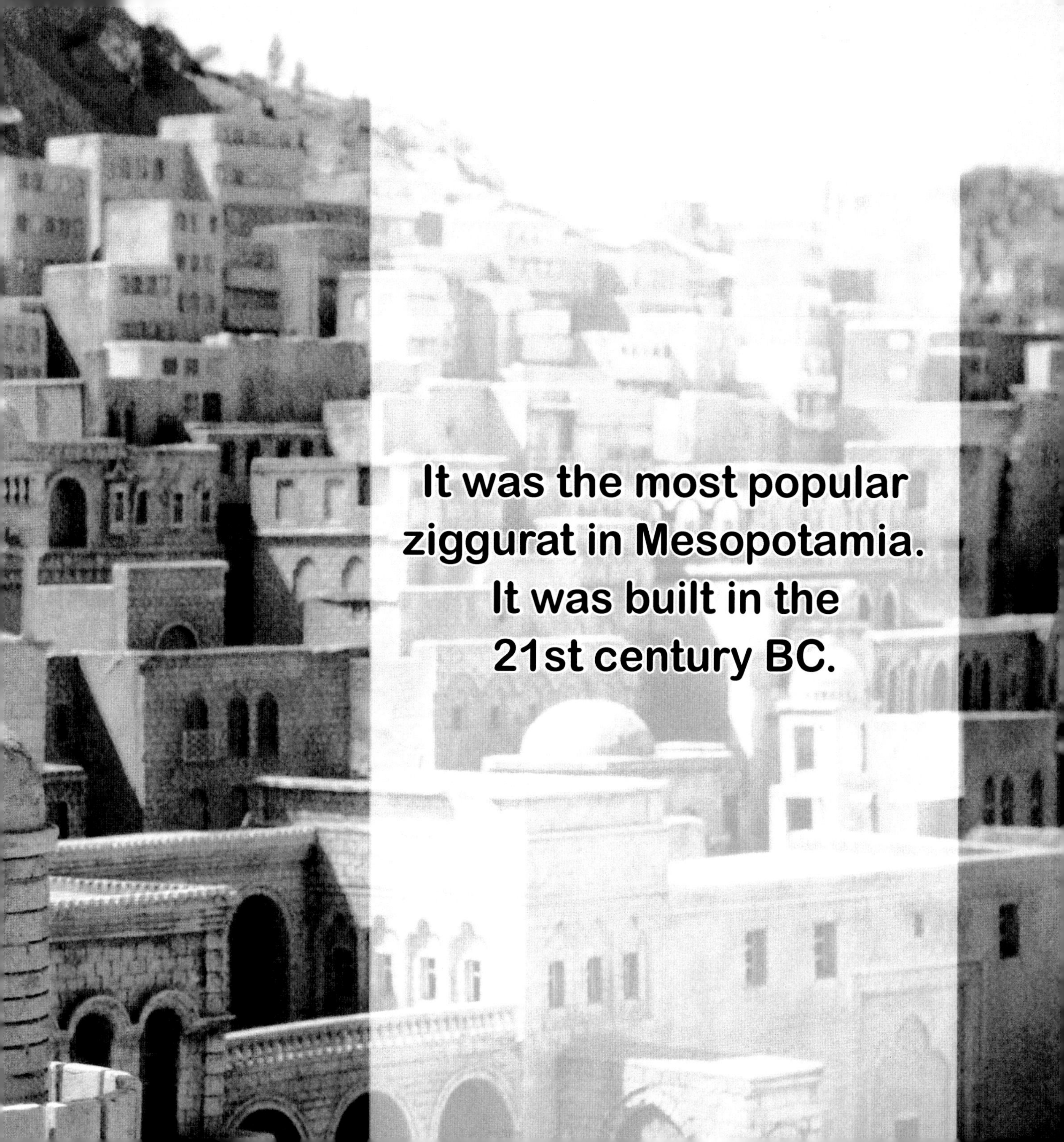

It was the most popular
ziggurat in Mesopotamia.
It was built in the
21st century BC.

Ziggurats were made of sun-dried mud bricks. If the structures got damaged, the kings would immediately have the ziggurats rebuilt.

By learning about ancient Mesopotamia, we can understand more about human civilization. We come to know the reasons why ancient Mesopotamia is known as the “Cradle of Civilization”.

There are more interesting facts about Mesopotamia. Research and have fun!

Visit
BABY PROFESSOR
EDUCATION KIDS
www.BabyProfessorBooks.com
to download Free Baby Professor eBooks and view
our catalog of new and exciting Children's Books

Made in the USA
Middletown, DE
20 April 2021

38014861R00038